WELCOME TO THE IMAGINARY AQUARIUM

Let's meet the adorable creatures that live here. They are all one-of-a-kind combinations of two animals!

Sunbra
sunfish + zebra

Climouse
clione + mouse

Elephin
elephant + dolphin

Squirrelotter
squirrel + sea otter

Whalesharkitty
whale shark + kitty

Dugosheep
dugong + sheep

Jellybear
jellyfish + bear

Kittyshark
kitty + shark

Sealster
seal + hamster

Octopiggy
octopus + piggy

Squidhog
squid + hog

Squiglet
squid + piglet

Turwolf
turtle + wolf

Mr. Zookeeper
polar bear + panda

Eelpuppy
eel + puppy

Kangalion
kangaroo + sea lion

Li'l Bunnyguin
baby bunny + penguin

Budgiseal
budgie bird + fur seal

Bunnyguin
bunny + penguin

**This is the outside of the aquarium.
What does the shape remind you of?**

Find and circle the pile of Sealster's sunflower seeds that is different from the others.

Answer on page 118

Follow the step-by-step instructions to draw Bunnyguin on the next page.

1

2

3

4

5

Turwolf can be shy, but not when teaching.
Then Turwolf can't wait to share ideas!

**Color these yummy treats
any way you like!**

Everyone remembers to brush before bedtime!

"U" IN THE AQUARIUM

Add the letter "u" to complete the names of these popular animals from the Imaginary Aquarium.

B_dgiseal

D_gosheep

S_nbra

T_rwolf

Answers on page 118

**Bunnyguin and Li'l Bunnyguin
are ready for a rainy day!**

Draw your favorite animal from the Imaginary Aquarium.

Make a check mark next to each animal or item below that you find in the picture.

Answers on page 118

Crunch, crunch! It's a beautiful day for a picnic at the Imaginary Aquarium.

Finish the drawing of Octopiggy using the grid as a guide. Then color the picture!

Lunchtime is munch time!

Whalesharkitty always has a smile for visitors.

It's almost showtime.
The Sealsters are ready to go!

Help Li'l Bunnyguin find Bunnyguin by following the trail of carrots!

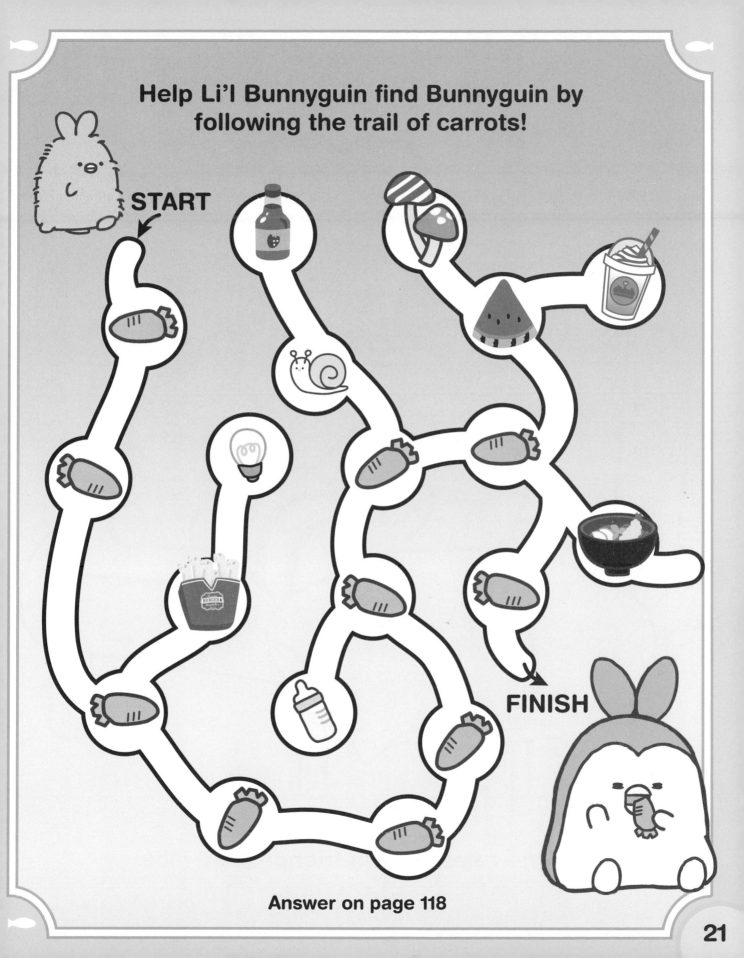

START

FINISH

Answer on page 118

Ahhh—relaxing with friends is so nice!

Bunnyguin is serving a delicious and colorful lunch.

The Imaginary Aquarium™

Connect the dots and color the train so the passengers can ride around the Imaginary Aquarium!

Answer on page 118

Mr. Zookeeper has scooped a yummy ice cream cone for Li'l Bunnyguin.

Turwolf and Sealster love their cold, sweet treats!

Bunnyguin and Li'l Bunnyguin are ready for a costume party!

Circle the two Budgiseal bunches that are exactly the same.

Answer on page 118

Li'l Bunnyguin is ready to give a special performance!

Follow the letters for the word
NURSERY
so Bunnyguin can pick up Li'l Bunnyguin.

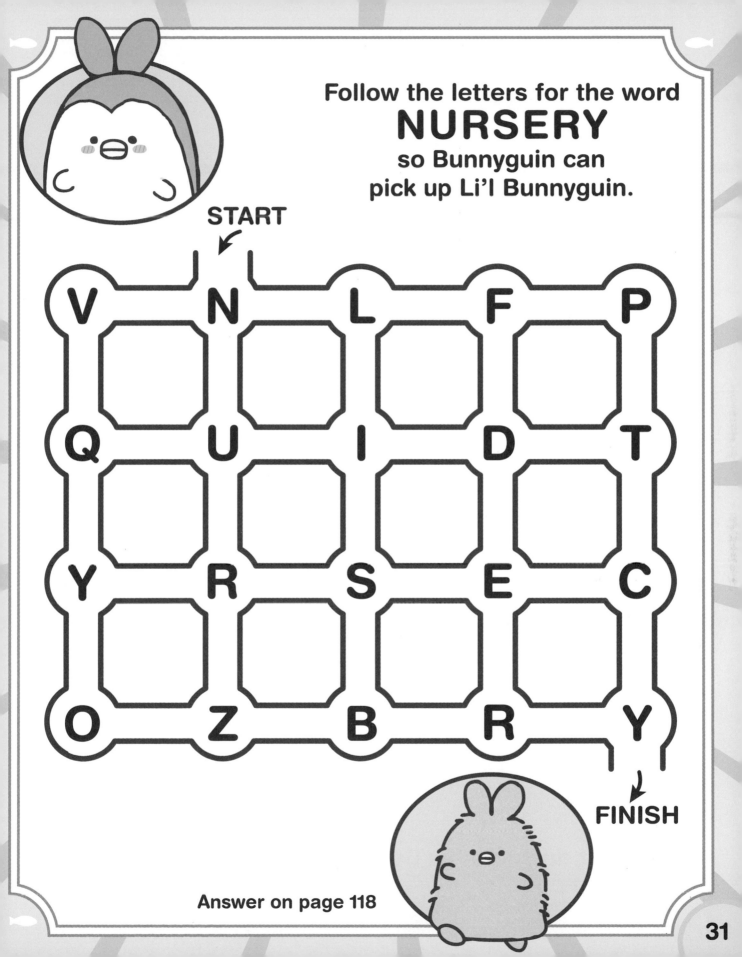

START

V   N   L   F   P

Q   U   I   D   T

Y   R   S   E   C

O   Z   B   R   Y

FINISH

Answer on page 118

What do you think Bunnyguin is reading about?

"Once upon a time, there was
a very special aquarium. . . ."

Two Elephin artists are creating a masterpiece!

Mr. Zookeeper is making a portrait of Turwolf.

You are invited to Budgiseal's barbecue!

Get Elephin to the ball as quickly as you can so the show can start!

START

FINISH

Answer on page 118

Circle the small picture of Octopiggy that matches the large picture exactly.

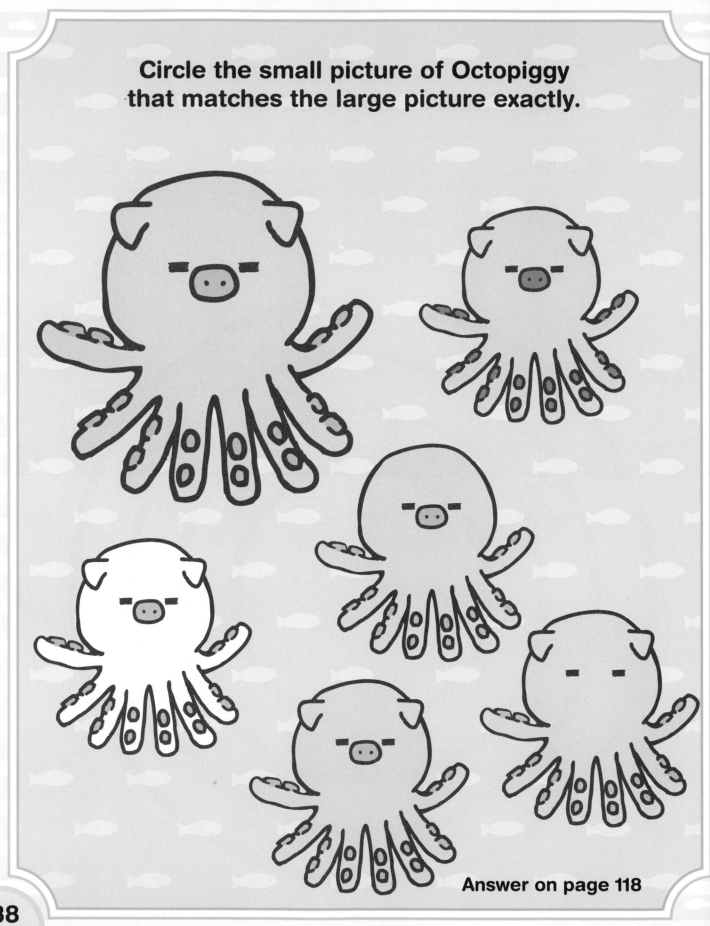

Answer on page 118

We're ready for dinner!

**Do you want to come in
from the cold and cuddle with us?**

**The Imaginary Aquarium friends love
to play in the snow!**

41

Make a check mark next to each animal or item below that you find in the picture.

Answers on page 118

**Homework is easier
when you do it with a friend.**

**The Bunnyguins are working on
an arts-and-crafts project.**

Help Li'l Bunnyguin get to the wading pool to go swimming with the Budgiseals!

START

FINISH

Answer on page 119

Splash!

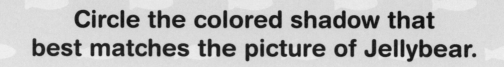

Circle the colored shadow that best matches the picture of Jellybear.

Answer on page 119

The Elephins are the stars of the show!

Draw yourself as an animal in the Imaginary Aquarium, and give yourself a name, too!

MY NAME IS

It's time for a photo shoot!

Everyone loves a Budgiseal chorus!

Baby Kangalion is growing beautiful plants!

Baby Kangalion is going to have some sweet cherries—with a little help from Mr. Zookeeper!

Li'l Bunnyguin and Baby Kangalion
are nature explorers today!

Welcome to Career Day at the Imaginary Aquarium!

Make a check mark next to the career you like best!

Circle the picture that is different in each row.

Answers on page 119

58

Beautiful Budgiseals make great friends.

What do you think Mr. Zookeeper ordered for lunch? Draw it on the table.

**Li'l Bunnyguin takes the stage
at the Imaginary Aquarium party!**

Squidhog and Octopiggy are
waiting for you to visit!

Squiglet loves doing homework!

**Take a good look at
the underwater ballet!**

"A" IS FOR AQUARIUM ANIMALS

Complete each animal's name by writing the letter "a" in the blank spaces.

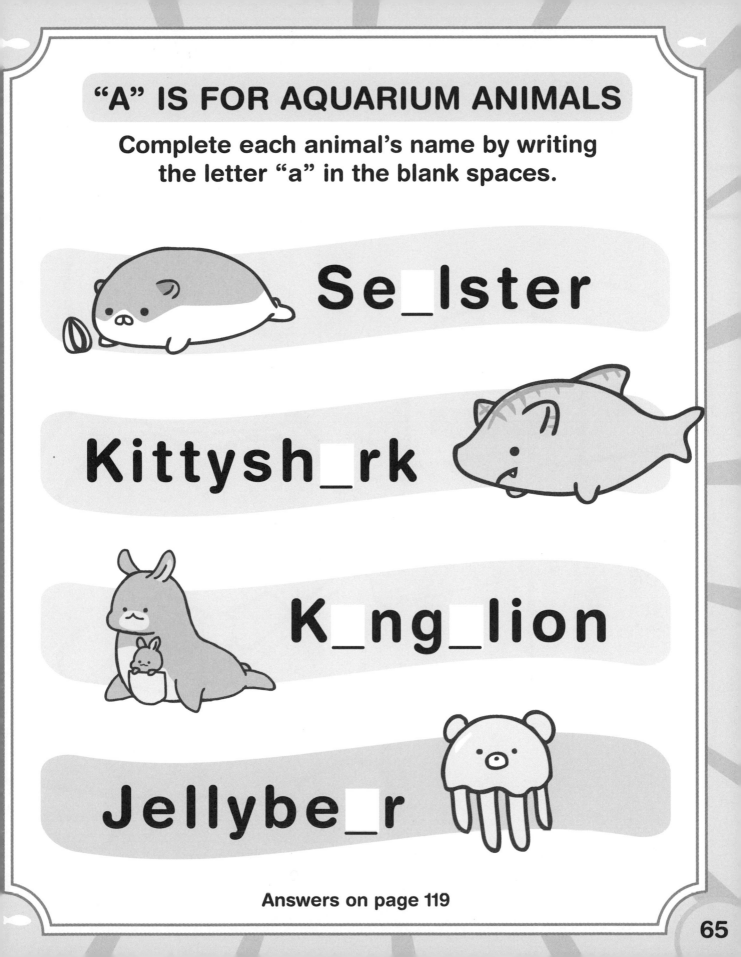

Se_lster

Kittysh_rk

K_ng_lion

Jellybe_r

Answers on page 119

Bunnyguin is delivering the mail.

Everyone gets a friendly letter!

It's time for a haircut!

**Friends like to have fun
swimming together.**

Circle the Climouse group
that is different from the others.

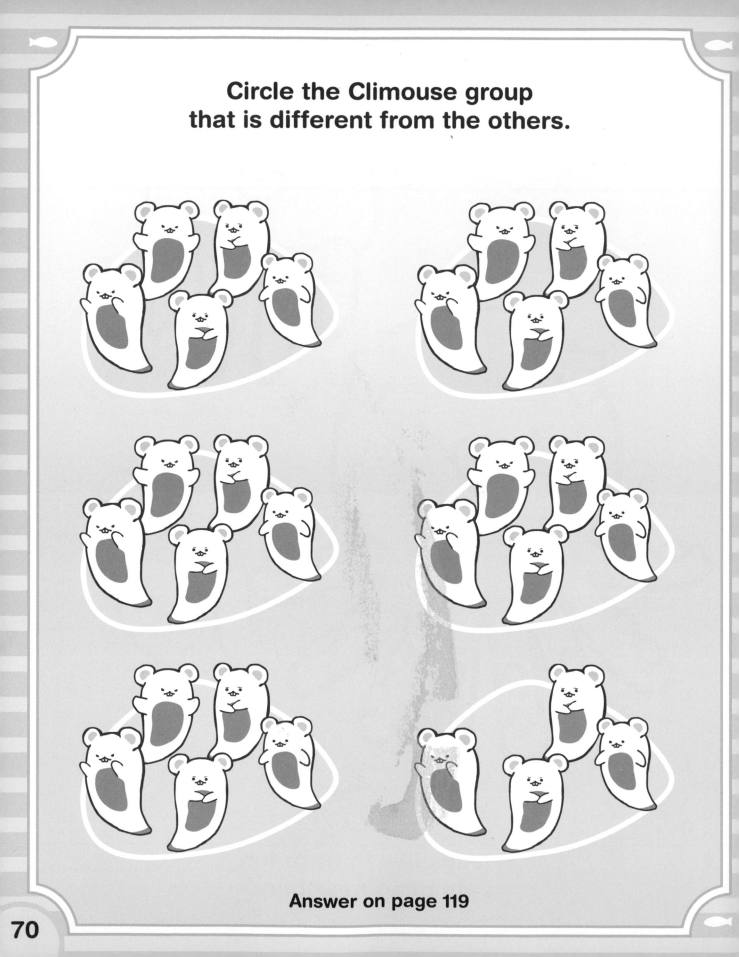

Answer on page 119

**Would you like to take a vacation
with the Bunnyguins?**

**There's always a friend nearby
at the Imaginary Aquarium!**

How many acorns does Squirrelotter have?
Write the answer on the line below.

_____

Answer on page 119

Dugosheep loves to knit!

Which outfit should Li'l Bunnyguin wear today?

Follow the step-by-step instructions to draw Whalesharkitty on the next page.

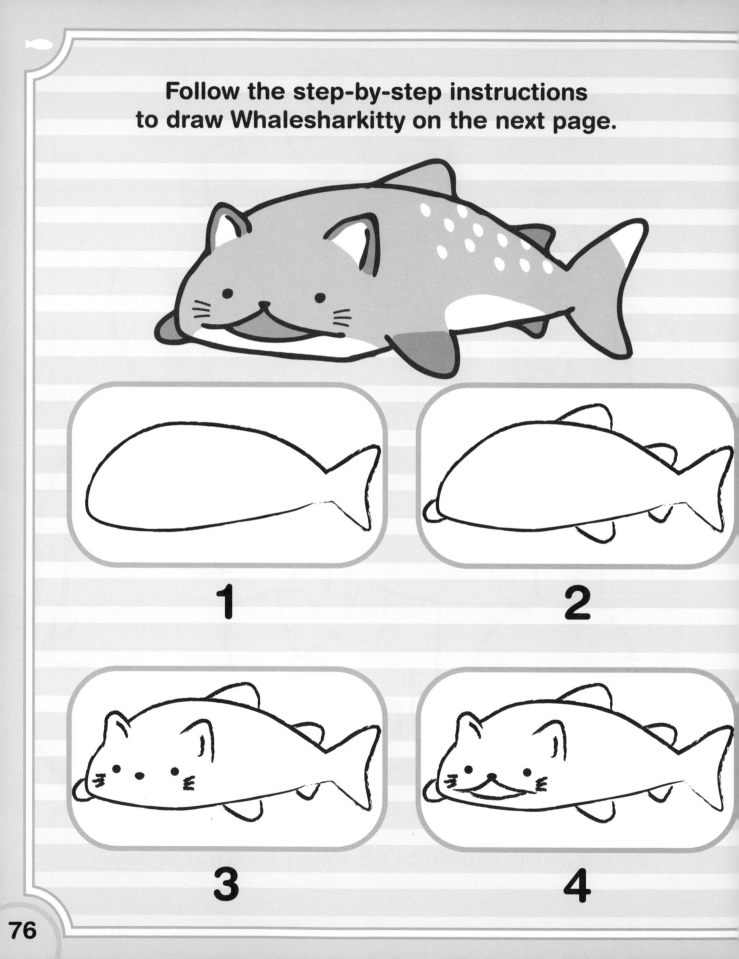

1

2

3

4

**Budgiseals stop talking long enough
to have a snack.** *Chomp!*

**Turwolf and friends share a lazy day
at the Imaginary Aquarium.**

Bunnyguin and Li'l Bunnyguin have
a sweet time together.

It's time for some skating fun!

Circle the picture that is different in each row.

Answers on page 119

**Everyone wears their finest clothing
for a very special visitor—you!**

Draw the friend you think Bunnyguin should give the box of chocolates to.

Match the baby to its parent.

Answers on page 119

How many Eelpuppy pairs are here?
Circle each pair you see.

Answer on page 119

Follow the step-by-step instructions to draw Mr. Zookeeper on the next page!

1

2

3

4

5

Octopiggy loves to make bowls and cups.

Time for school!

Baby Kangalion wants to show love
to Kangalion with a flower.
Help the baby deliver the gift.

START

FINISH

Answer on page 119

There are more than enough presents to go around!

Bunniguin, Li'l Bunniguin, Budgiseal, and Sealster enjoy a fun swim together.

Get Octopiggy and Squidhog back to the Imaginary Aquarium in time for lunch!

START →

FINISH →

Answer on page 119

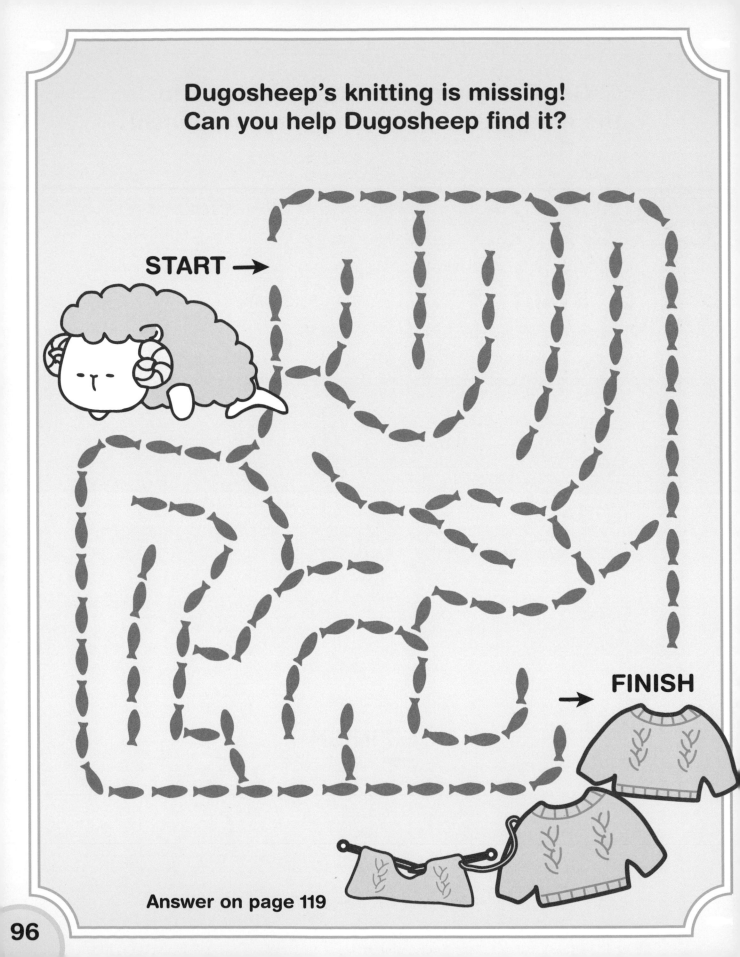

Dugosheep's knitting is missing!
Can you help Dugosheep find it?

START →

FINISH

→

Answer on page 119

Even the coldest part of the Imaginary Aquarium
is warm when you're with friends!

Finish the drawing of Squidhog using the grid as a guide. Then color the picture!

What colors would look good for Budgiseal?

It's time for the Imaginary Aquarium Olympics!

Everyone's a winner!

Make a check mark next to each animal or item below that you find in the picture.

Answers on page 120

Circle the picture that is different in each row.

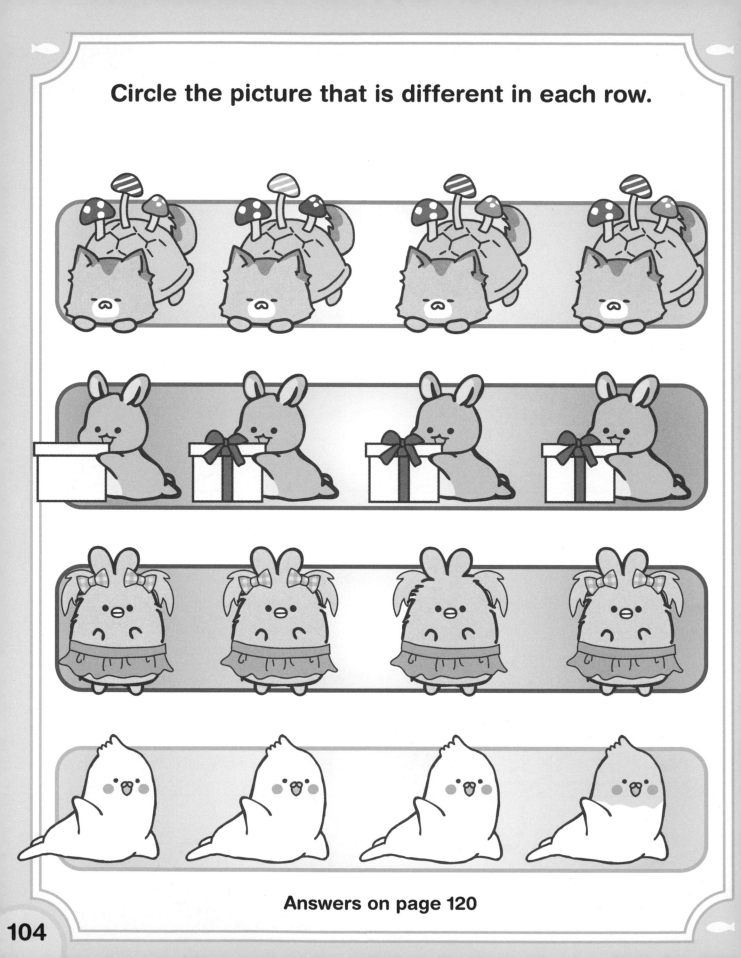

Answers on page 120

Look—it's the first Bunnyguin on the moon!

Everyone exercises to stay in great shape!

Connect the dots so Bunnyguin can wave to you!

Answer on page 120

Circle nine carrots in this dinner party scene.

Answers on page 120

**Do you want to take a dip in
the ocean with these friends?**

Connect the dots and color the umbrella so Li'l Bunnyguin can stay dry.

Answer on page 120

Draw a line between each stylish outfit and the Bunnyguin who is wearing it!

Answers on page 120

Connect the dots so Squidhog can help Squiglet do the homework.

Answer on page 120

Bunnyguin and Budgiseal pitch in to help clean the Imaginary Aquarium after it closes for the day.

Everyone gets cozy and
listens to a bedtime story.

Sweet dreams! Tomorrow's another fun day at the Imaginary Aquarium!

ANSWERS

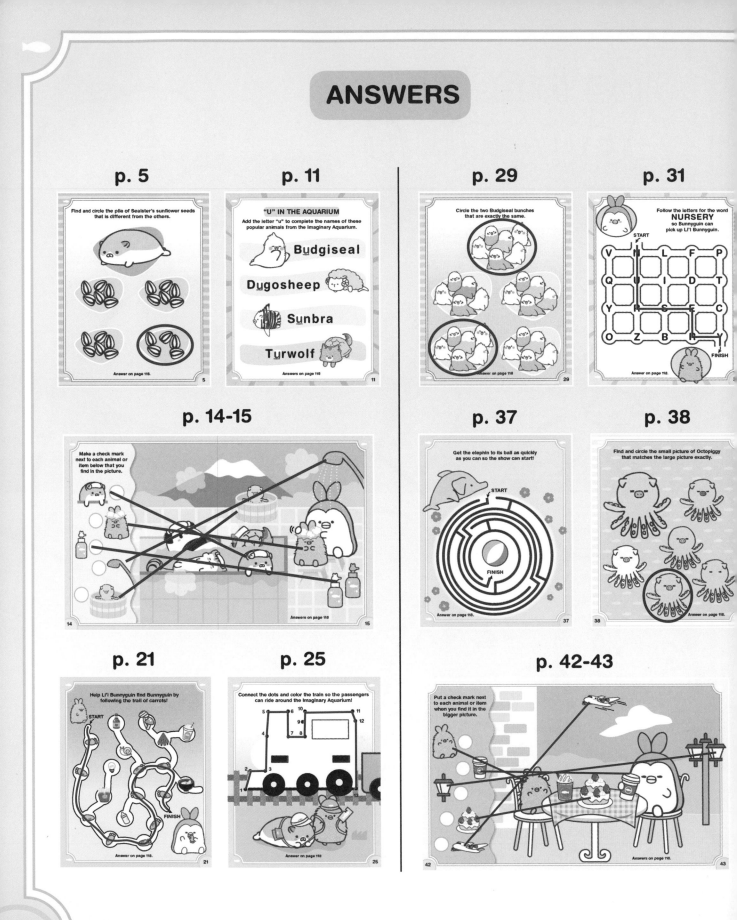

p. 5

Find and circle the pile of Seaister's sunflower seeds that is different from the others.

Answer on page 118.

5

p. 11

"U" IN THE AQUARIUM

Add the letter "u" to complete the names of these popular animals from the Imaginary Aquarium.

B**u**dgiseal

D**u**gosheep

S**u**nbra

T**u**rwolf

Answers on page 118

11

p. 14-15

Make a check mark next to each animal or item below that you find in the picture.

14

Answers on page 118

15

p. 21

Help Li'l Bunnyguin find Bunnyguin by following the trail of carrots!

START

FINISH

Answer on page 118.

21

p. 25

Connect the dots and color the train so the passengers can ride around the Imaginary Aquarium!

Answer on page 118

25

p. 29

Circle the two Budgiseal bunches that are exactly the same.

Answer on page 118

29

p. 31

Follow the letters for the word **NURSERY** so Bunnyguin can pick up Li'l Bunnyguin.

START

FINISH

Answer on page 118.

31

p. 37

Get the elephin to its ball as quickly as you can so the show can start!

START

FINISH

Answer on page 118.

37

p. 38

Find and circle the small picture of Octopiggy that matches the large picture exactly.

Answer on page 118.

38

p. 42-43

Put a check mark next to each animal or item when you find it in the bigger picture.

42

Answers on page 118.

43

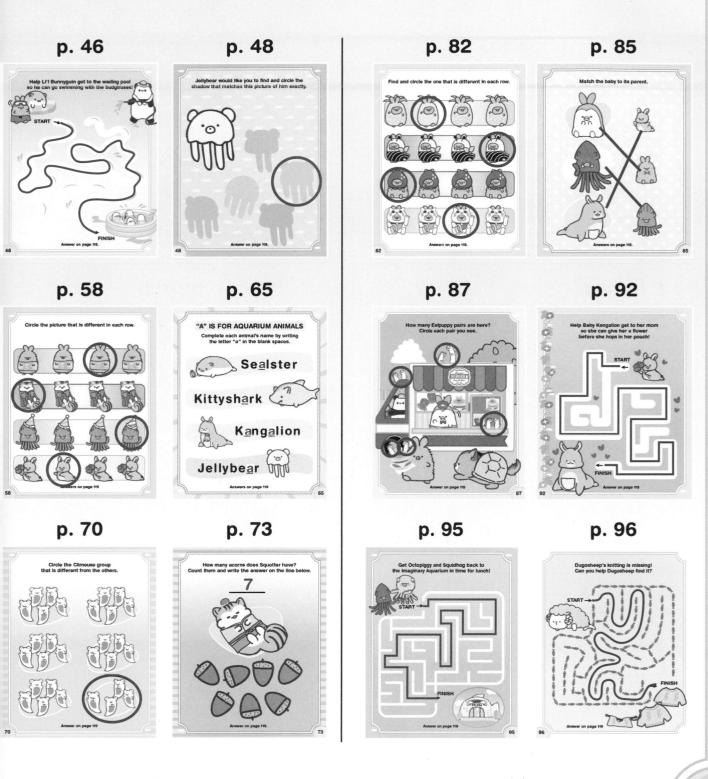

p. 46

Help Li'l Bunnyguin get to the wading pool so he can go swimming with the budgiruses!

START

FINISH

Answer on page 118.

p. 48

Jellybear would like you to find and circle the shadow that matches this picture of him exactly.

Answer on page 118.

p. 82

Find and circle the one that is different in each row.

Answers on page 118.

p. 85

Match the baby to its parent.

Answers on page 118.

p. 58

Circle the picture that is different in each row.

Answers on page 119

p. 65

"A" IS FOR AQUARIUM ANIMALS

Complete each animal's name by writing the letter "a" in the blank spaces.

Se**a**lster

Kittysh**a**rk

K**a**ng**a**lion

Jellybe**a**r

Answers on page 119

p. 87

How many Eelpuppy pairs are here? Circle each pair you see.

BURGERS

Answer on page 119

p. 92

Help Baby Kangalion get to her mom so she can give her a flower before she hops in her pouch!

START

FINISH

Answer on page 119

p. 70

Circle the Climouse group that is different from the others.

Answer on page 119

p. 73

How many acorns does Squotter have? Count them and write the answer on the line below.

7

Answer on page 119.

p. 95

Get Octopiggy and Squidhog back to the Imaginary Aquarium in time for lunch!

START

FINISH

Answer on page 119

p. 96

Dugosheep's knitting is missing! Can you help Dugosheep find it?

START

FINISH

Answer on page 119

ANSWERS

p. 102-103

p. 111

p. 104

p. 107

p. 112-113

p. 108-109

p. 114